COOKING
FOR BEGINNERS

Roz Denny and Fiona Watt

Designed by Mary Cartwright
Illustrated by Kim Lane
Photography by Howard Allman

Food preparation by Ricky Turner and Lizzie Harris
Cover illustration by Christyan Fox

Contents

Before you begin

Before you begin to cook any of the recipes in this book, read through these two pages and pages 4-5. They will give you lots of tips about cooking.

Equipment

The first thing you need to do is read through the recipe you are planning to cook. This is to make sure that you have all the equipment you will need.

Sharp knife

Serrated knife

Slotted spoon

Wooden spoon

Colander

Potato peeler

Strainer

Kitchen scissors

Brush

Spatula

Garlic press

Measuring cup

Grater

Large mixing bowl

Chopping board

Oven mitts

Baking sheet

Your oven

Arrange the shelves in your oven before you turn it on to the heat it says. If you have a fan oven, read its instruction book and reduce the heat, or the cooking time, by the amount the book suggests.

Ingredients

Before you start to cook, make sure that you have all the ingredients in the list at the beginning of the recipe. Ingredients are shown by weight and by using cups and spoons. Those shown by weight are generally sold that way.

Using caution

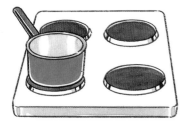

When you are using a saucepan or frying pan, always make sure that the handle is turned to the side of your stove.

Be careful that you don't touch anything hot. Wear oven mitts whenever you put dishes into, or take them out, of your oven.

Don't leave your kitchen while you're cooking on the stove burners. Always turn off your oven, burners, or broiler when you finish.

Measuring with a spoon

If you don't have special measuring spoons, you can use regular spoons. Measure the ingredient as a level spoonful, not heaped up above the edge of the spoon, unless you are told to.

Soup spoon *A tablespoon*

Teaspoon

A level spoon

A heaped spoon

3

Cooking hints

These two pages explain the cooking words and skills which appear in the recipes in this book. Read through them before you start to cook.

Breaking an egg

Crack the shell by tapping an egg sharply on the rim of a cup or a bowl. Push your thumbs into the crack and pull the shell apart.

Sifting

1. You sift an ingredient to get rid of any lumps. Place your strainer over a large bowl and spoon in the correct amount.

2. Lift the strainer slightly and shake it from side to side. You may need to use a spoon to push the last bit through the strainer.

Adding salt and pepper

Try adding a pinch of salt and three or four 'twists' of a peppermill.

In some recipes you will find that it says to add some salt and pepper. The amount you add depends on your own taste.

Beating a mixture

Before you begin to beat a mixture, put a damp dishcloth under your bowl. This stops the bowl from slipping as you beat.

Briskly stir the ingredients together with a wooden spoon or whisk, until they make a smooth, creamy mixture.

Making stock

Crumble a bouillon cube into a measuring cup, then pour boiling water into the cup. Stir it with a spoon until the cube dissolves.

Peeling potatoes

Wash your potatoes in cold water, first.

Hold a potato in one hand, then scrape a potato peeler away from you again and again to remove all the skin.

Grating cheese

Cut a piece of cheese which weighs more than you need. Grate some, then weigh the grated cheese. Grate more if you need to.

A garlic bulb   *A clove of garlic*

Preparing garlic

Some of the recipes in this book include garlic. A clove of garlic is one of the sections of a whole bulb.

1. To remove a clove of garlic from the bulb, squeeze and twist the bulb until you split the outer layers of skin.

2. Slice a small piece off the top and bottom of the clove, then peel off its skin. The garlic is now ready to crush.

Using a garlic press

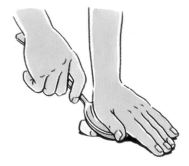

1. Put a clove of garlic inside a garlic press, like this. Close the press and squeeze the handles together tightly.

2. Run the blade of a knife over the holes on the press, to scrape off any crushed garlic which is still sticking to it.

If you don't have a garlic press, put a clove of garlic under the back of a spoon. Push down firmly on the clove several times.

Chopping an onion

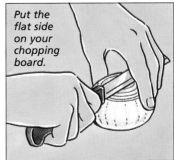

Put the flat side on your chopping board.

1. Put the onion onto a chopping board. Use a vegetable knife to cut off the top and the bottom. Be careful as you cut.

2. Run your knife around one side to slice the skin. Lift a piece of the skin at the cut, then peel the rest of it off the onion.

3. Hold the onion like this and cut it in half. Put the cut side onto the chopping board and chop each half as finely as you can.

Tomato and mozzarella salad

Serves 4

4 large ripe tomatoes
4 tablespoons of olive oil
salt and ground black pepper
10oz. mozzarella cheese
8 large fresh basil leaves

Use a serrated knife.

Core

1. Cut the tomatoes in half and cut the core out of each one. Lay each half on its flat side and slice them as finely as you can.

2. Arrange the tomatoes on four plates. Trickle a tablespoon of oil over each one. Sprinkle on a little salt and some black pepper.

3. If your mozzarella is in a bag full of liquid, slit the bag and pour the liquid away. Cut the mozzarella into thin slices.

4. Lay the slices of mozzarella among the tomatoes. Tear the basil leaves into thin strips and sprinkle them on.

5. Cover the plates with plastic food wrap and leave them in your refrigerator for about 30 minutes, then serve.

Summer salad

Serves 4

1 small crispy head of lettuce
half a cucumber
1 large carrot
3 green onions
a tub of alfalfa sprouts

For the dressing:
3 tablespoons of olive oil
1 tablespoon of white wine vinegar
1 teaspoon of clear honey
a pinch of dried mixed herbs
a pinch of salt and ground black pepper

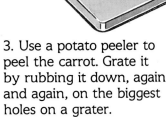

1. Cut the end of the stalk off the lettuce. Pull the leaves off, wash and tear into bite-sized pieces. Put them into a large bowl.

2. Cut the cucumber in half lengthwise. Scrape out the seeds with a teaspoon. Cut each half into thin slices.

3. Use a potato peeler to peel the carrot. Grate it by rubbing it down, again and again, on the biggest holes on a grater.

4. Add the cucumber and carrot to the lettuce. Cut the roots and tops off the green onions. Slice them into ¾ inch pieces.

5. Add the onions to the lettuce. Use kitchen scissors to snip the sprouts from the tub. Add them to the bowl.

6. Put all the ingredients for the dressing into a jelly jar. Screw on its lid and shake it well. Pour the dressing over the salad.

Leek and potato soup

Serves 4

2 medium potatoes
2 medium leeks
2 tablespoons butter
1 tablespoon of cooking oil
1 vegetable bouillon cube
dried bouquet garni
1¼ cups of milk
small handful of fresh parsley
salt and ground black pepper

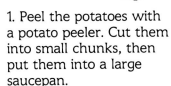

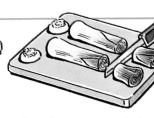

1. Peel the potatoes with a potato peeler. Cut them into small chunks, then put them into a large saucepan.

2. Cut the roots and the dark green tops off the leeks. Slice through the outside layer and peel it off each leek.

Stir the vegetables occasionally.

3. Wash the leeks thoroughly under cold, running water. Make sure that there is no dirt left in the layers.

4. Cut across the leeks so that you get ½inch slices. Put the slices into the pan and add the butter and oil.

5. Turn on the heat and slowly melt the butter. When it starts to sizzle, put a lid on the pan and turn the heat down low.

Stir until the bouillon cube dissolves.

6. Let the vegetables cook gently for ten minutes. Shake the pan occasionally to stop it from sticking, but don't lift the lid.

7. Meanwhile, boil some water. Put the bouillon cube into a measuring cup. Pour in 4 cups of boiling water and stir it.

8. When the vegetables are cooked, carefully pour in the stock. Add a pinch of bouquet garni, the milk and a little salt and pepper.

Chopping parsley

Stir it occasionally.

9. Turn up the heat and bring the mixture to a boil. Then, turn the heat down so that the mixture is bubbling gently.

10. Let the soup cook for 15 minutes, until the leeks and potatoes are soft. Ladle it into bowls and sprinkle it with chopped parsley.

Put the parsley into a mug. Use scissors to snip the parsley into fine pieces. It is easier than using a knife.

Cheesy beef burgers

Serves 4

1lb. lean ground beef
2 tablespoons light soy sauce
1 teaspoon dried bouquet garni
ground black pepper
1½ oz. Cheddar cheese
sunflower oil

Make sure that
your hands are clean.

1. Remove the broiler pan
and rack from your
broiler and put it to one
side. Turn your broiler on
to its highest setting.

2. Put the ground beef into
a bowl. Break it up with a
fork. Add the soy sauce,
herbs and two 'twists' of
black pepper (see page 4).

3. Mix the ingredients
well and divide it in four.
Squeeze each lump of
mixture into a round. flat
shape (see tip, right).

Press the cheese into the
middle.

4. Cut the cheese into four
cubes. Press a cube into
each burger. Push the
mixture over to
cover the cheese.

You could serve
your burgers
with oven fries
and salad.

You could serve your burgers in brown or white buns with lettuce and slices of tomato. Add a little mayonnaise too, if you like.

5. Fold a paper towel several times and pour a little oil onto it. Wipe it across the rack of your broiler pan.

Space the burgers out evenly on the broiler rack.

6. Use a spatula to lift the burgers onto the broiler rack. Turn the heat down to medium and cook the burgers for seven minutes.

7. After seven minutes, turn the burgers over, by sliding a spatula under each one and holding the top with a fork.

8. Cook the burgers for seven minutes more. Check that they do not become too brown. Turn the heat down a little if they are.

9. Press a fork on a burger to test it. If you like medium-cooked burgers they will feel springy. Well-done ones feel firm.

Tip: shaping burgers

Dip your hands in clean, cold water to stop the mixture from sticking to your hands when you shape it.

Creamy fish pie

Serves 4

1lb. 2oz. of boneless, skinless white
fish fillet (e.g. cod or haddock)
1¾ cups milk
bouquet garni
salt and ground black pepper

4 medium potatoes
2 tomatoes
4 green onions
2 tablespoons of soft margarine
2 tablespoons of flour
1 cup frozen peas, defrosted

Watch the pan in case the milk boils over.

1. Put the fish into a saucepan. Pour in the milk, along with a pinch of bouquet garni, some salt and black pepper.

2. Bring the milk to a boil, then turn the heat down low so that it is bubbling very gently. Cook it for five minutes.

3. Take the pan off the heat. Lift out the fish with a spatula, but don't throw away the milk. Leave the fish to cool.

4. Meanwhile, peel the potatoes. Cut them into chunks. Put the chunks into a pan and cover them with cold water.

5. Add half a teaspoon of salt and bring the water to a boil. Turn down the heat so that it bubbles gently. Put a lid on the pan.

6. Cook the potatoes for 10-15 minutes until they are soft. While they are cooking, use a fork to break the fish into flakes.

Slice across the onions.

7. Cut the tomatoes into small chunks. Cut the roots and the green tops off the green onions and slice the onions finely.

8. When the potatoes are cooked, drain them in a colander over a sink. Put the chunks back into the pan, but not on any heat.

9. Crush the potato by pressing a potato masher down, again and again, on the chunks. Do it until there are no lumps left.

Mix it with a wooden spoon.

10. Add two tablespoons of milk from the fish pan and a tablespoon of butter, to the potato. Mix it well.

Turn the heat down to let it bubble gently.

11. Mix the flour with a little milk. Stir it into the milk, with a tablespoon of butter. Boil it, then let it bubble gently for one minute.

12. Add the fish, onion, peas and tomatoes. Cook for two minutes. Pour the mixture into an ovenproof dish. Turn on your broiler to medium.

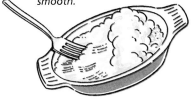

Use a fork to make the top of the potato smooth.

13. Spoon the potato on top. Put the dish under the broiler. Cook it until the potato becomes golden. Serve it immediately.

Crunchy cheese omelette

For one person

1½ oz. mature Cheddar or Gruyère cheese
6 stems of fresh chives or 3 sprigs of fresh parsley
2 tablespoons of mini croutons
2 large eggs
salt and ground black pepper
2 teaspoons of olive oil

Look for mini croutons in the soup or snack section of a supermarket.

1. For the filling, grate the cheese on the coarse side of the grater (see page 4). Put the grated cheese into a small bowl.

2. Use kitchen scissors to snip the chives or parsley into the bowl. If you are using parsley, don't chop the thick part of the stalk.

3. Use your fingers or a knife to break the croutons into pieces, about the size of peas. Add them to the bowl and mix well.

You could add sliced tomato and basil instead of the croutons.

Page 4 shows you how to break an egg.

4. Break the eggs into another bowl. Add a tablespoon of water and a little salt and pepper. Beat them well.

You could serve your omelette with some lettuce.

5. Heat a small non-stick frying pan over a medium heat for a minute without anything in it. Then, add the oil.

The egg will set a little on the bottom.

6. Heat the oil for a few seconds. Carefully tilt the pan so that the oil coats the base of it. Pour in the egg and let it cook a little.

Hold the pan handle in one hand.

7. Use a non-metal spatula to pull the egg away from the side of the pan. Tip the pan to let runny egg flow into the space.

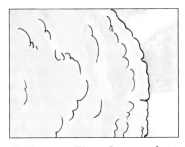

8. Keep pulling the omelette away from the side of the pan until all the runny egg is cooked. The top should still look creamy.

9. Spoon the filling all over the top. Tilt the pan at an angle and use a spatula to fold over one half of the omelette.

10. Leave the filling to cook for a few seconds. Turn off the heat. Slide the omelette onto a plate and eat it immediately.

Stuffed crêpes

Serves 4, makes about 12 crêpes

1 cup all-purpose flour
a pinch of salt
1 egg
sunflower oil
1¼ cups of milk

For the filling: 1 tablespoon of sunflower oil
14oz. lean ground beef or turkey
11oz. jar of tomato pasta sauce
5oz. of sour cream
2oz. grated Cheddar cheese

1. Put a strainer over a large mixing bowl. Pour in the flour and the salt. Shake the strainer until all the flour has fallen through.

Put a dishcloth under the bowl to stop it from slipping.

2. Press a whisk into the middle of the flour to make a deep hollow. Break an egg into a cup, then pour it into the hollow.

Use a whisk.

3. Add a tablespoon of oil and two tablespoons of milk. Beat the egg, oil and milk with some of the flour from around the hollow.

The mixture will make a smooth batter.

Brush the oil quickly over the bottom of the pan.

4. Add some more of the milk and beat it again. Continue to add some milk and beat it, until all the milk is mixed in.

5. Heat a small frying pan over medium heat for about a minute. Don't put anything into the pan at this point.

6. Put two tablespoons of oil into a cup. Fold a paper towel in half and roll it up. Dip one end into the oil and brush it over the pan.

The batter should sizzle.

7. Put the batter next to your pan. Quickly add three tablespoons of batter. Swirl it all over the bottom by tipping the pan.

8. Put the pan flat on the heat and cook it until the batter turns pale and is lightly cooked. Small holes will also appear on top.

9. Loosen the edge of the crêpe and slide a spatula under it. Flip the crêpe over and cook it for half a minute more.

Make a stack of crêpes under the dish towel.

10. Slide the crêpe onto a plate then cover it with a clean dish towel. Repeat steps 6-11 until the batter is finished.

11. Heat a tablespoon of oil in a saucepan. Add the meat. Break it up with a wooden spoon and cook it until it is brown all over.

12. Stir the pasta sauce into the meat. Bring the pan to a boil then turn it down so that it bubbles gently. Cook for five minutes.

Fill each crêpe in the same way.

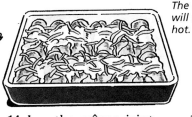

The dish will be hot.

13. Lay a crêpe on a plate. Spoon on two tablespoons of mixture. Fold one side over the mixture, then roll it up.

14. Lay the crêpes, joint-side down in an ovenproof dish. Turn on your broiler. Spoon on the cream and sprinkle cheese on top.

15. Put the dish under the broiler. Leave it until the cheese starts to bubble and turns golden brown. Serve immediately.

Crusty bread 'pizzas'

Serves two

1 ciabatta bread,
or 1 thick French stick

For the topping; 1 onion
2 cloves of garlic
2 tablespoons of olive oil
$14\frac{1}{2}$ oz. can of chopped tomatoes
half a teaspoon of dried bouquet garni
salt and ground black pepper
9oz. of mozzarella cheese
2 tablespoons of grated Parmesan cheese

Stir it once or twice.

1. Cut the top and bottom off the onion and peel it. Cut it in half and slice it. Peel the garlic cloves and crush them (see page 5).

2. Heat two tablespoons of oil in a frying pan. Gently cook the garlic and onion, for five minutes, or until they are soft.

3. Add the tomatoes, the herbs and some salt and pepper. Turn up the heat and bring the mixture to a boil.

You could put olives or slices of salami or ham on top of the cheese, before you cook them.

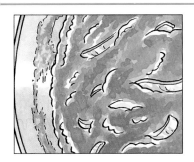

4. Turn the heat down to medium and let the topping cook for about ten minutes, or until most of the liquid has gone.

5. Take the pan off the heat. Leave the mixture to cool for 10-15 minutes. Turn your oven on to 400°F.

6. Put your bread onto a chopping board and carefully cut it in half lengthwise. Put each half onto a large baking sheet.

7. Spread each piece of bread with the topping. Slice the mozzarella cheese as finely as you can and lay the slices on top.

8. Sprinkle the Parmesan cheese on top. Bake the 'pizzas' for about 15 minutes or until the cheese is bubbling.

9. Take the baking sheet out of the oven and let the bread cool for five minutes. Cut each half into pieces, to make it easier to eat.

Try one with cheese, pepperoni and olives.

Cheesy spinach quiche

Serves 4

12oz. ready-made pie crust, thawed
    if frozen

8oz. fresh leaf spinach

1 onion

2 cloves of garlic

1 tablespoon of olive oil

2 cups grated Cheddar cheese

2 medium eggs

¾ cup half and half or whole milk

salt and ground black pepper

an 8 inch quiche pan or baking dish

Heat your oven to 325°F.

Make sure that your work surface is clean and dry.

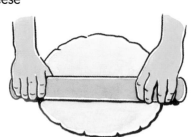

1. Sprinkle a little flour on your work surface and onto a rolling pin. Shape the pie crust into a smooth, round ball.

2. Roll the pie crust, turn it in a quarter turn and roll it again. Keep on doing this until you get a circle about 10in. across.

3. Put your pan or dish onto a baking sheet. Roll the pie crust over the rolling pin then unroll the pie crust onto the dish.

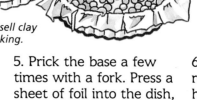

Some stores sell clay beans for baking.

4. Press the pie crust into the base and up the sides of the dish, without tearing it. Bring the pie crust over the rim of the dish.

5. Prick the base a few times with a fork. Press a sheet of foil into the dish, then fill the base with dried beans.

6. Put the crust into the refrigerator for half an hour. Turn on your oven. Wash the spinach and put the leaves into a large pan.

Press the water out of the spinach with the back of a spoon.

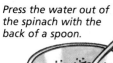

Wear oven mitts.

7. Cook the spinach for three minutes over medium heat. It wilts as it cooks. Drain it; press out the water. Leave it to cool.

8. Slice the onion and crush the garlic (see page 5). Put the oil into a pan. Cook the onion and garlic for five minutes, until they are soft.

9. When the pie crust has cooled, put it into the oven. Cook it for 15 minutes, then lift it out of the oven carefully.

10. Lift off the foil and the beans. Trim off the pie crust around the rim. Put the crust, uncovered, in the oven for five more minutes.

11. Turn your oven to 325°F. Spread the onion mixture over the crust. Cut up the spinach and add it too.

12. Sprinkle the cheese and a little salt and pepper on top of the spinach. Beat the eggs with the cream or milk, in a small bowl.

13. Pour the mixture over the filling. Put the quiche into the oven for about 30 minutes or until the top has set and is golden.

Pan-fried meat or fish

Serves 4

2 tablespoons of olive oil
either: 4 x 4oz. sirloin or rump steaks,
   or 4 skinless, boneless chicken breasts,
   or 4 x 4oz. skinless, boneless salmon fillets
2 sprigs of fresh parsley
salt and black pepper

1. If you are using chicken breasts, make two cuts on top of each one with a sharp knife. Put four plates in a warm place.

2. Put a non-stick frying pan onto a burner and turn it on to a high heat. Leave it for a minute without anything in it.

3. Pour the oil into the pan and brush it over the bottom. Add the pieces of steak, chicken or salmon. They will sizzle a little.

4. If you are cooking steak, cook the pieces on one side for two minutes, or for three to four minutes if you like them well done.

If chicken is cooked, the juices are clear, not pink.

If you are using chicken, cook the pieces for four to five minutes on one side. Chicken should always be well-cooked.

It makes it tastier if you let it stand.

For salmon, cook the pieces for about three minutes on one side. The fillets should still be a little juicy and not dry.

5. When you have cooked the pieces on one side, turn the heat to medium. Turn them over and cook them for the same time again.

6. When the meat or fish is cooked, use a spatula to lift it onto the warm plates. Let them stand for few minutes.

This piece of chicken was cooked in a special skillet. The browned stripes are made by the ridges on the skillet.

7. Chop the parsley (see page 9) and sprinkle a little onto each piece. Serve the meat or fish with potatoes and a salad.

Lamb kebabs in pitta pockets

Serves 4

2 large lamb leg steaks, about 6 oz. each
1 clove of garlic
half a teaspoon of mild curry powder
1 tablespoon of oil
4 wooden kebab sticks
small head of leaf lettuce
half of a cucumber
2 tablespoons of natural yogurt
1 teaspoon of dried mint, or
1 tablespoon of fresh chopped mint
salt and ground black pepper
2 large pitta breads

You can squeeze some lemon juice onto the lamb before you serve it.

1. If there is a small bone in the middle of the lamb steaks, cut it out. Cut the meat into cubes, with sides about ¾ inch.

2. Peel and crush the garlic (see page 5). Put the garlic, curry powder, oil and a little salt and pepper into a bowl and mix well.

3. Add the meat into the bowl and stir it well. Cover the bowl with plastic foodwrap and leave it for half an hour.

4. Put the wooden sticks into a bowl of cold water and leave them to soak. This stops them from burning under the broiler.

Throw away the core of the lettuce.

5. Shread the lettuce by cutting across it and put it in a bowl. If you are using fresh mint, chop the leaves finely.

6. Cut the cucumber in half, then slice it finely. Mix the lettuce, yogurt, mint and cucumber, with a little salt and pepper.

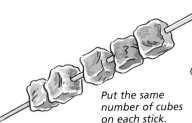

Put the same number of cubes on each stick.

7. Turn your broiler on to medium. Dry the kebab sticks on a paper towel, then push the cubes of lamb onto them.

8. Put the kebabs onto the broiler rack and push it under your broiler. Cook the kebabs for five minutes, then turn them over.

9. Cook the kebabs for five minutes more. While they are cooking, cut the pitta bread in half across the middle, like this.

10. Put the kebabs on a plate. Put the pittas under the broiler for two minutes but turn off the heat. This will warm them through.

11. Run the tip of a knife along the cut edge of each pitta to open it up. Fill each one with some of the lettuce mixture.

12. Hold a kebab stick at one end and use a fork to slide the lamb off. Put some lamb into each pitta and eat immediately.

Vegetable stir fry

Serves 4

1 carrot
1 red or yellow pepper
2 zucchinis
4oz. snow peas
4 green onions
4oz. baby corn
1 clove of garlic
4oz. fresh bean sprouts
2-3 tablespoons of vegetable oil

For the sauce:
1 teaspoon of cornflour
1 tablespoon of light soy sauce
2 tablespoons of water
2 tablespoons of oil
a pinch of sugar

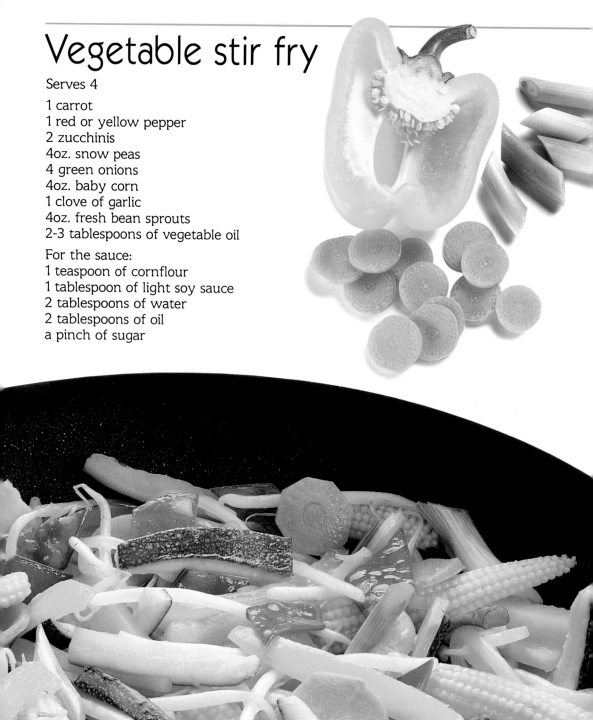

It's easiest to slice a pepper from the inside.

Cut the pieces about 2in. long.

1. Peel the carrot with a potato peeler. Cut off the top and bottom, then slice it into circles, as finely as you can.

2. Cut the pepper in half. Cut out the stalk and scrape out the seeds and white pieces inside. Cut it into thin slices.

3. Cut the ends off the zucchinis. Cut them in half lengthwise. Slice the halves into strips then cut them into shorter pieces.

4. Snip the ends off the snow peas using a pair of kitchen scissors. Then, cut each snow pea into smaller pieces, with a knife.

5. Cut the roots and the dark green ends off the green onions. Peel the outer layer off them, then slice them diagonally.

6. Cut the ends off the baby corn, then cut them in half lengthwise. Peel the clove of garlic and crush it (see page 5).

These vegetables were cooked in a special stir-fry pan, but you can use a large frying pan or a wok.

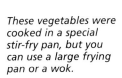

Stir quickly with a wooden spoon or spatula.

7. Put the cornflour into a cup and add a few drops of water. Mix it to make a paste. Stir in the rest of the sauce ingredients.

8. Heat two tablespoons of oil in a frying pan or wok. Add the carrot, pepper and zucchini to the pan. Cook them for three minutes.

Stir the vegetables as they cook.

9. Add the corn, garlic and onions. Cook them for a minute. Add the snow peas and bean sprouts. Cook the mixture for three minutes.

10. Stir the sauce in the cup then quickly pour it into the pan. Stir it to coat the vegetables and serve them immediately.

Pasta with fresh tomato sauce

Serves 4

For the sauce: 8 medium tomatoes
2 cloves of garlic
3 tablespoons of olive oil
half a teaspoon of sugar

Pasta shapes such as shells, twists or spirals are best for this recipe.

12oz. dried pasta shapes
1 tablespoon of olive oil
salt and ground black pepper
12 fresh basil leaves

To serve: grated Parmesan cheese

Use a slotted spoon.

1. Boil some water. Pull any stalks off the tomatoes. Use the tip of a knife to cut an 'X' on the bottom of each tomato.

2. Put the tomatoes into a heat-proof bowl. Carefully pour the boiling water over the tomatoes so that they are covered.

3. Leave the tomatoes for at least a minute. Fill another bowl with cold water, then spoon the tomatoes into it.

4. Lift the tomatoes out of the water. Use your fingers to peel off their skins, starting at the cuts you made.

5. Cut each tomato into quarters, then cut out the tough cores. Cut the fleshy part of each tomato into small pieces.

6. Peel the garlic and crush it (see page 5). Heat the oil in a large saucepan. Add the tomatoes, garlic and sugar and stir well.

7. Turn the heat to medium and cook the sauce for about five minutes. Stir it once or twice as it cooks.

8. While the sauce is cooking, fill a large pan with water and put it on to boil. Add a teaspoon of salt to the water.

9. When the water is boiling hard, add the pasta and stir it once or twice. Bring the pan back to a boil.

When you serve your pasta, sprinkle it with the grated Parmesan cheese.

Drain the pasta in a colander over a sink.

Add a little salt and pepper too.

10. Turn down the heat so the water is bubbling, but not too fiercely. Turn the heat under the sauce as low as it will go.

11. Cook the pasta for the time it says on its package, then drain it. Rinse the pasta under cold water. Put it back into its pan.

12. Add a tablespoon of oil to the pasta and stir in the sauce. Rip the basil leaves into pieces and stir them in. Serve immediately.

Shrimp and pepper curry

Serves 4

7oz. peeled, cooked shrimp
1 medium onion
1 clove of garlic
1 red or yellow pepper
2 tablespoons of oil
1 tablespoon of butter
1 tablespoon of mild curry powder
1¼ cups of basmati rice
1¾ cups of water
⅓ cup of shredded coconut
1 teaspoon of salt
1 cup of peas
freshly ground black pepper

1. If you are using frozen shrimp, spread them out on a plate. Leave them for two hours to defrost, then drain them in a colander.

2. Cut the ends off the onion, peel the onion and cut it in half. Slice each half finely then cut the slices into small pieces.

3. Peel the garlic clove and crush it (see page 5). Cut the red or yellow pepper in half. Cut out the seeds and the stalk.

4. Slice the pepper finely, then cut the slices into small pieces. Make them about the same size as the pieces of onion.

Stir it occasionally.

5. Heat the oil and butter gently in a large non-stick pan. Add the vegetables. Cook them on a medium heat for seven minutes.

6. Stir in the curry powder and add the rice. Add the coconut to the pan along with the water and salt.

Stir it once or twice.

7. Turn up the heat and bring the mixture to a boil. When it has boiled, turn the heat down so that it is bubbling gently.

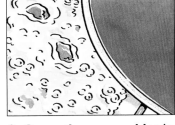

8. Cover the pan and let it cook for ten minutes. Don't lift the lid while it is cooking as the steam in the pan cooks the rice.

Add a little black pepper too.

Stir it to separate the grains of rice.

9. Remove the lid carefully and stir in the shrimp and peas. Put the lid on the pan again and cook it for two to three minutes.

10. Take the pan off the heat and leave it, with the lid on, for five minutes. Stir the mixture with a fork and serve immediately.

Beef goulash with linguini

Serves 4

1 bouillon cube
1 onion
2 cloves of garlic
1 red or yellow pepper
1lb. braising beef
2 tablespoons of sunflower oil or olive oil
1 teaspoon of dried bouquet garni
1 tablespoon of paprika

1 tablespoon of wine vinegar
14½oz. can of chopped tomatoes
7oz. linguini pasta
1 tablespoon of butter or soft margarine
5oz. sour cream
salt and ground black pepper

Heat your oven to 325°F.

Stir the meat as it cooks.

1. Make 1¼ cups of stock (see page 4). Cut the ends off the onion and peel off the skin. Cut it in half and slice it finely.

2. Peel and crush the garlic. Cut the pepper in half and remove the core and the seeds. Slice it finely. Turn on your oven.

3. Cut the meat into ½ inch chunks. Heat the oil in a frying pan over a medium heat. Add the meat and start to cook it.

Add a little salt and pepper too.

4. When the chunks of meat have browned all over, remove the meat with a slotted spoon and put it on a plate.

5. Put the onion, garlic and pepper into the pan. Stir them well and cook them for five minutes, until they are soft.

6. Sprinkle on the herbs and paprika. Put the meat back in the pan and stir it. Add the vinegar, tomatoes and the stock.

Wear oven mitts.

7. Bring the mixture to a boil, stirring it as it cooks. Once it has boiled, ladle it carefully into an oven-proof dish. Put a lid on the dish.

8. Put the dish into the oven for an hour. Take it out and stir it. Put the lid back and return it to the oven for half an hour.

9. About 20 minutes before the meat is ready, fill a large pan with water. Add a teaspoon of salt and bring the water to a boil.

10. Put the pasta into the water and bring back to a boil. Turn the heat down so that it isn't boiling too hard.

11. Cook the pasta for the time it says on its package, then drain it in a colander. Spoon the butter onto the pasta and toss it.

12. Put the pasta onto four plates or bowls and put the meat onto top. Add some sour cream on top.

Cooking pasta

This shows yellow egg linguini, but you could use green spinach linguini for this dish.

When you cook pasta, start measuring its cooking time from when the water boils again after adding the pasta.

Roast chicken and vegetables

Serves 4

1 roasting chicken, about 4lbs., defrosted if frozen
2 tablespoons of oil
1 teaspoon of dried bouquet garni
1lb. new potatoes
2 medium onions, preferably red onions
1 red pepper
1 green or yellow pepper
2 tablespoons of sour cream
salt and ground black pepper

Heat your oven to 375°F.

Scrub the potatoes first if they are not clean.

1. Turn on your oven. Untie the legs of the chicken. Either pull off, or cut out, the fatty pads inside the chicken's body.

2. Place the chicken in a roasting pan. Rub a tablespoon of oil over the skin. Sprinkle it with herbs and some salt and pepper.

3. Put the potatoes into a clean plastic bag. Add a tablespoon of oil. Rub the potatoes so that they become coated with oil.

Don't cut the bottom off the onions.

4. Put the potatoes into the pan, around the chicken. Put the chicken into the oven and cook it for 45 minutes.

5. Meanwhile, cut the onions in quarters and peel off their skin. Cut the peppers into quarters and cut out the core and seeds.

6. Toss the onion and pepper pieces in the oily plastic bag. Add them to the pan when the chicken has cooked for 45 minutes.

7. So that the chicken browns evenly, put it back into the oven the other way around. Cook it for another 45 minutes.

8. After 45 minutes, scoop out the vegetables and put them in a serving dish. Put the dish into the oven, with the heat turned off.

9. Poke a knife into the meat beside a leg, to see if it is cooked. There should be no pink. If there is, cook it for five to ten more minutes.

Push a large spoon inside the chicken to lift it.

Pour the creamy juices over the pieces of chicken.

10. Lift up the chicken and hold it over the roasting pan and let the juices drip into it. Then put the chicken onto a plate.

11. Turn a burner onto a low heat and put the pan on top. Cook the juices for a minute, then stir in the sour cream.

12. Pull the legs and thighs off the chicken and cut the rest of the meat off with a sharp knife. Serve it with the vegetables.

Lemon and honey cheesecake

Serves 6

9oz. large graham cracker squares
4oz. butter
two 3oz. packages of lemon gelatin
    mix or 4½oz. package of
    concentrated gelatin
5 tablespoons of clear honey
10oz. heavy cream
7oz. sour cream
an 8in. quiche or pie pan with a loose
base. It should be about 1½in. deep.

Use the
back of a
spoon to
press the
crumbs.

1. Put the crackers into a clean plastic bag. Seal the bag with a rubber band. Roll a rolling pin over the crackers to crush them.

2. Melt the butter in a saucepan over a low heat. Pour in the cracker crumbs from the bag and mix them with the butter.

3. Grease inside of the pan with some butter. Spread the crumbs over the bottom. Press them to make a firm base.

4. Chill the base in a refrigerator. Pour the gelatin mix into a measuring cup or cut up the concentrated gelatin.

5. Warm a tablespoon under a hot tap (see tip, below). Dry it and add five tablespoons of honey to the gelatin mix.

6. Pour 1¼ cups of boiling water into the cup. Stir the mixture well, until the gelatin dissolves. Leave the mixture to cool.

7. Meanwhile, put the cream into a large bowl. Use a wooden spoon to beat in the sour cream until it is smooth.

8. When the gelatin mixture is cool, pour it into the bowl with the creamy mixture. Beat it hard with a whisk to mix it well.

9. Pour the creamy mixture into the pan. Put it carefully into the refrigerator and leave it for about four hours to set.

Measuring honey

10. When the cheesecake is firm, lift it onto a can. Carefully press down on the sides of the pan to loosen the base.

11. Leave the cheesecake on the pan's base. Put it onto a plate and leave it in a fridge until you are ready to eat it.

Warm your spoon under a hot faucet before you dip it into a jar of honey. This makes it easier to measure.

Spiced apple crumble

Serves 4

3-4 eating apples
6 tablespoons of water
ground allspice
1 tablespoon of sugar

For the topping: 1 cup of all-purpose flour
1 cup of whole-wheat flour
¾ cup of sunflower margarine or butter
⅔ cup of light soft brown sugar

Heat your oven to 350°F.

1. Cut the apples in quarters, peel them. Cut out the cores. Cut the quarters into chunks. Put them in a medium casserole dish.

2. Add the water. Sprinkle the apples with a large pinch of allspice and a tablespoon of sugar. Turn on your oven.

3. Stir the two kinds of flour together in a bowl. Cut the margarine or butter into small pieces and add it to the flour.

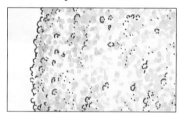

4. Wash your hands and dry them well. Rub in the margarine or butter into the flour using your fingers (see the tip, right).

5. When the mixture looks like coarse breadcrumbs, mix in the brown sugar. Mix it in with your fingers too.

6. Sprinkle the topping over the apple. Spread it out and smooth it with the back of a fork. Put the dish onto a baking sheet.

Wear oven mitts.

7. Bake the crumble for 45 minutes, until the top is golden. Turn the crumble around halfway through, so that it browns evenly.

8. Push the tip of a knife into a piece of apple. If it's not soft, put the crumble back into the oven for five more minutes.

9. Leave the crumble for at least five minutes to cool a little before you serve it. Serve it with ice cream.

You could use plums or blackberries instead of apples.

Rubbing in

Use a blunt knife to mix the pieces of margarine or butter. Stir and cut the flour until the pieces are coated with flour.

Rub the pieces between your fingertips. As you rub, lift the mixture up and let it drop. It will mix to look like breadcrumbs.

Strawberry trifle

Serves 4

1lb. fresh strawberries
4 short cakes (or sponge cake)
2 tablespoons of raspberry or strawberry jam
4 tablespoons of apple juice
1 small lemon
1¼ cups of heavy cream
3 tablespoons of milk
half a teaspoon of vanilla extract
2 tablespoons of sugar

1. Pull the stalks out of the strawberries. Try to pull them out with the white core attached. Use a small knife to help you.

Leave a few strawberries for the top of your trifle.

2. Cut most of the strawberries in half, or in quarters if they are big. Put the pieces into a medium-sized bowl.

3. Cut the cakes in half. Spread each half with jam then press them back together again. Cut the cakes into quarters.

Grate just the skin, not the white part beneath.

4. Put the pieces of cake on top of the strawberries and mix them gently. Trickle the apple juice over them.

5. Cover your bowl with plastic food wrap and put it into your refrigerator for about three hours. The cakes will turn soft.

6. Grate the yellow skin, or zest, from the lemon, using the medium holes on a grater. Use a knife to scrape off the zest.

Spread the cream with the back of a spoon.

7. When the cake mixture is nearly chilled, put the cream into a large bowl. Add the milk, lemon zest, vanilla and sugar.

8. Beat the mixture with a whisk until it forms soft peaks. If you beat it too much, it will become too solid to spread.

9. Lightly spread the creamy mixture over the cakes and strawberries. Put it in the refrigerator until you are ready to serve it.

Gooey chocolate fudge cake

Serves 6-8

2 teaspoons of sunflower oil
1¾ cups of self-rising flour
6 tablespoons of cocoa powder
2 teaspoons of baking powder
1½ cups of sunflower margarine
    (not low fat spread)
2¼ cups of soft brown sugar

2 teaspoons of vanilla extract
6 large eggs
5oz. dark baking chocolate
⅔ cup of milk
1½ cups of powdered sugar
¼ cup of butter

two 8 inch round cake pans

Heat your oven to 325°F.

Cut just inside the line you have drawn.

Use a pastry brush.

1. Turn on your oven. Put the cake pans onto wax paper and draw around them. Cut out the circles.

2. Brush sunflower oil over the inside of the pans. Put a paper circle inside each one and brush the top of it with oil.

3. Sift the flour, cocoa and baking powder into a bowl (see page 4). Put another large bowl onto a damp dishcloth.

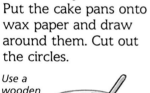

Use a wooden spoon.

Don't forget to add a tablespoon of flour with each egg.

This cake is best if it is eaten on the day you make it.

4. Put the margarine and sugar into the empty bowl and beat them until they are creamy. Add the vanilla and beat it again.

5. Crack one egg into a cup. Add it to the bowl with one tablespoon of flour. Beat it well. Repeat this with each egg.

Change to a metal spoon.

Spread the top level with a knife.

6. Gently stir in the rest of the flour, moving the spoon in the shape of a number eight. This keeps the mixture light.

7. Put the mixture into the cake pans. Put them on the middle shelf of the oven. Cook for 40 to 45 minutes. Test them (see page 45).

Run the knife around the edge again if it doesn't come out.

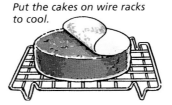

Put the cakes on wire racks to cool.

Use a heatproof bowl.

8. Wear oven mitts to lift the pans from the oven. Let them cool for five minutes, then run a knife around the sides of each pan.

9. Turn each pan upside down over a wire rack and shake it. The cakes should pop out. Peel off the paper and leave them to cool.

10. For the frosting, break the chocolate into a bowl. Add the milk and butter. Heat 2in. of water in a pan until it is just bubbling.

Put the cake on a plate.

11. Put the bowl in the pan. Stir the chocolate as it melts. When it has melted, add the sugar. Let it cool, then put it into a refrigerator.

12. Stir the frosting a few times while it is cooling. It will thicken. When it is like soft butter, take it out of the refrigerator.

13. Spread a third of the frosting on one cake. Put the other cake on top of it and cover the top and sides with your frosting.

Carrot cake

Serves 8-12 slices

a little oil for greasing
3 medium carrots
¾ cup margarine
1¼ cups light soft brown sugar
2 large eggs
1⅔ cups of self-rising flour
half a teaspoon of salt
2 teaspoons of ground cinnamon
2 teaspoons of baking powder

1 cup raisins
¾ cup chopped walnuts
2 tablespoons of milk

For the frosting: 7oz. cream cheese
1 tablespoon of lemon juice
2 cups powdered sugar
half a teaspoon of vanilla extract

an 8 inch round cake pan

Heat your oven to 350°F.

1. Put your cake pan onto a piece of wax paper and draw around it. Cut out the circle, just inside the line you have drawn.

2. Brush the sides and the base of pan with a little oil to grease it. Put the paper circle inside and brush this with oil, too.

3. Turn your oven on. Wash the carrots and cut off their tops. Grate them on the side of the grater with the biggest holes.

Put the bowl on a damp cloth.

4. Put the margarine into a saucepan and heat it slowly until it has just melted. Pour it into a large bowl.

5. Break the eggs into a small bowl and beat them. Stir the carrots and sugar into the margarine. Then, add the beaten eggs.

6. Put a strainer over the bowl. Shake the flour, salt, cinnamon and baking powder through the strainer, onto the mixture.

Push it in the middle.

7. Use a wooden spoon to beat the mixture, until it is smooth. Mix in the raisins and walnuts, then stir in the milk.

8. Spoon the mixture into the pan. Smooth the top with a spoon. Tap the pan on your work surface to make the mixture level.

9. Bake the cake for an hour. Test it by sticking a skewer into it. When it comes out it should have no mixture sticking to it.

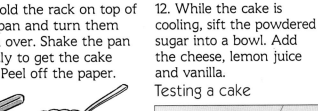

10. Put the cake pan on a wire rack and leave it for ten minutes. Then, run a knife around the side of the cake.

11. Hold the rack on top of the pan and turn them both over. Shake the pan gently to get the cake out. Peel off the paper.

12. While the cake is cooling, sift the powdered sugar into a bowl. Add the cheese, lemon juice and vanilla.

Testing a cake

13. Beat the mixture well. When the cake has cooled completely, cut it in half. Spread one piece with half of the frosting.

14. Put the other half of the cake on top. Spread the top of it with frosting Make swirly patterns on it with a fork.

Push a skewer or a sharp knife into the middle of the cake. If the cake is cooked, it will come out clean.

Tasty cookies

Makes about 60 small cookies. This recipe shows you how to make fruit cookies. See the labels for other flavors.

1¾ cups all-purpose flour
quarter of a teaspoon of salt
2 teaspoons of baking powder
1 large egg
¾ cup butter
1 cup sugar
1 teaspoon of vanilla extract
1 orange and 1 lemon

Heat your oven to 400°F.

You can add all kinds of things to these cookies. Try 2oz. of chopped nuts instead of the orange and lemon zest.

1. Measure the butter and leave it for about an hour to soften. Sift the flour, salt and baking powder into a bowl (see page 4).

2. Break the egg into a cup. Beat it briskly with a fork, so that the yolk and the white are mixed well together.

3. Put the butter and sugar into another bowl and beat them until they are creamy. Stir in the egg and vanilla.

Scrape the zest off the grater with a knife.

4. Grate the skin, or zest, off the orange and lemon using the medium holes on your grater. Stir it into the creamy mixture.

5. Add the flour and stir it until you get a smooth dough. If the dough feels very soft, put it into your refrigerator for an hour.

Orange and lemon cookies.

6. Put a long piece of foil onto your work surface and scrape the dough onto it. Roll the dough to make a long sausage shape.

For chocolate cookies, add two tablespoons of cocoa powder. Sift it in with the flour.

Use four tablespoons of shredded coconut instead of the zest to make coconut cookies.

7. Wrap the foil around the dough and put it in your refrigerator for about an hour, until it becomes firm. Turn on your oven.

8. Take the dough out of the refrigerator and cut it into thin slices. You don't need to use all the dough at one time (see the tip).

Storing the dough

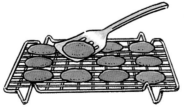

9. Spread out the slices of dough on a non-stick baking sheet. Bake them for about seven minutes, until they are golden.

10. Leave the cookies on the baking sheet for a minute. Using a spatula, slide them onto a wire rack to cool.

Wrap spare dough in foil. It will keep for about ten days in a refrigerator or up to six weeks in a freezer.

Index